TEEN TITANS GO!®

Raintree

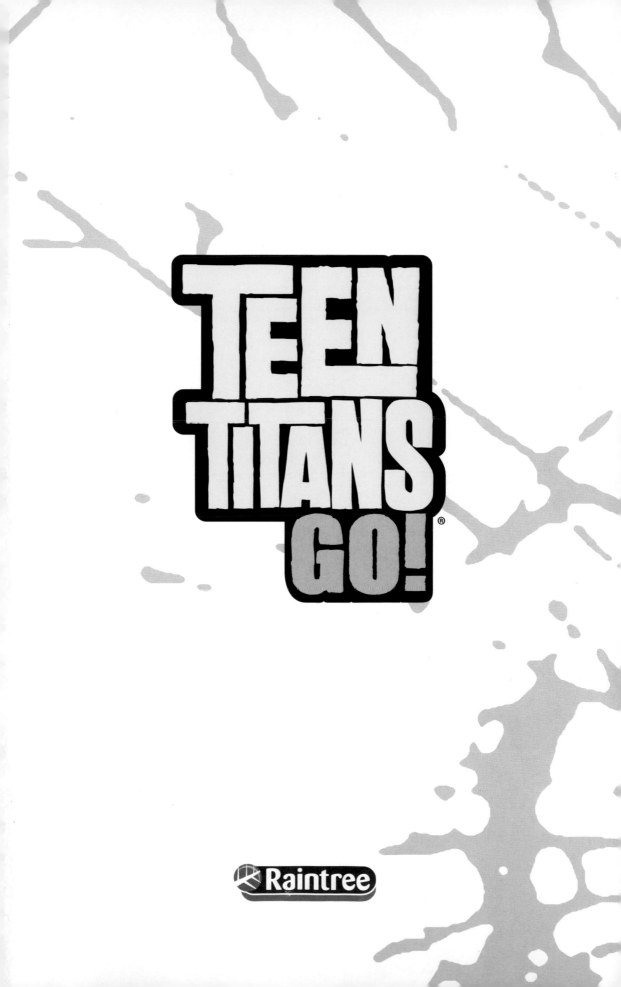

Raintree is an imprint of Capstone Global Library Limited, a company incorporated in England and Wales having its registered office at 7 Pilgrim Street, London, EC4V 6LB - Registered company number: 6695582

www.raintreepublishers.co.uk
myorders@raintreepublishers.co.uk

First published by Raintree in 2014
The moral rights of the proprietor have been asserted.

Ashley C. Andersen Zantop *Publisher*
Michael Dahl *Editorial Director*
Sean Tulien *Editor*
Heather Kindseth *Creative Director*
Alison Thiele *Designer*
Kathy McColley *Production Specialist*

DC COMICS
Kristy Quinn *Original U.S. Editor*

ISBN 978 1 406 27945 0

Printed in China by Nordica.
1013/CA21301918
17 16 15 14 13
10 9 8 7 6 5 4 3 2 1

A full catalogue record for this book is available from the British Library.

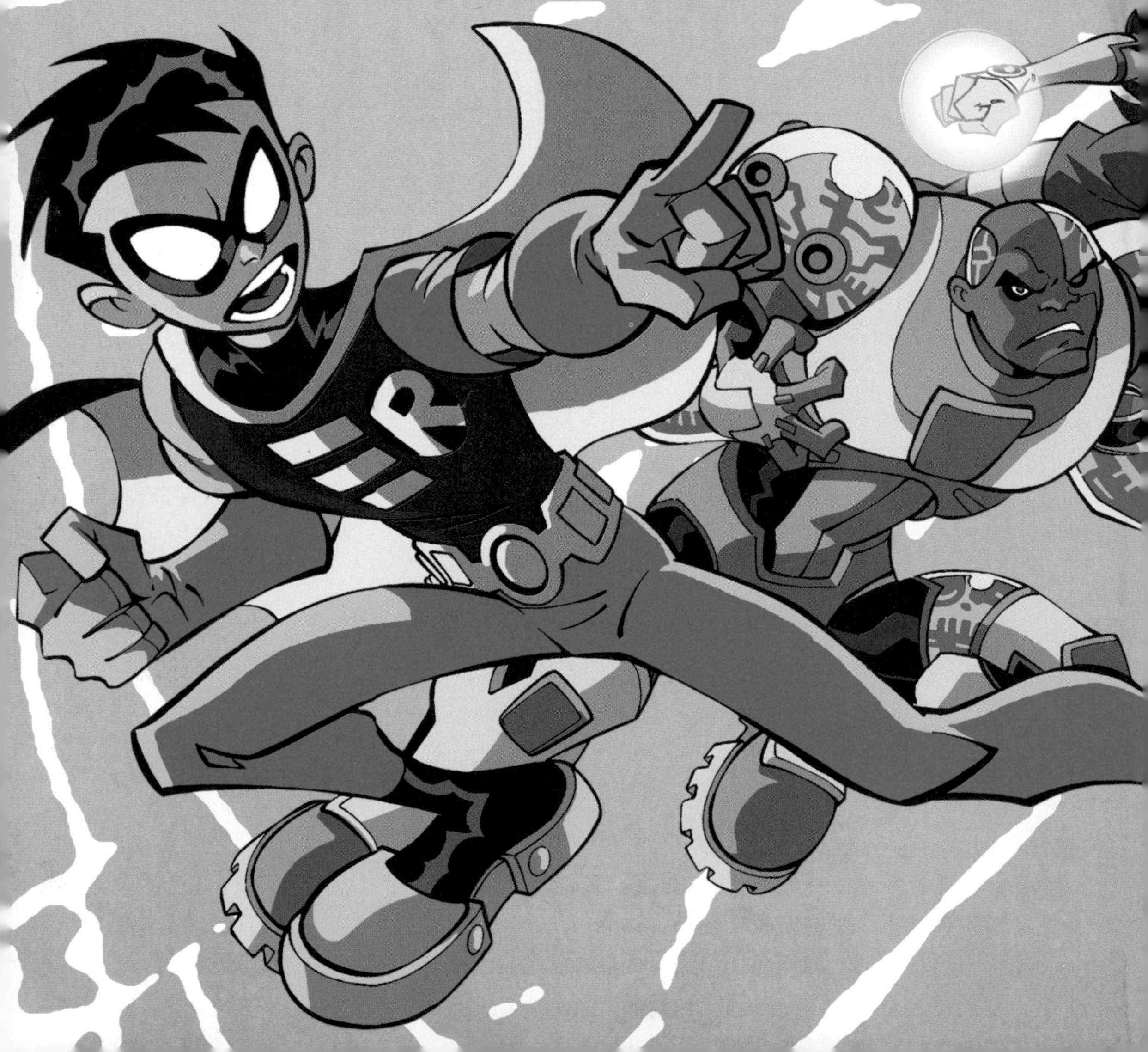

TEEN TITANS GO!®

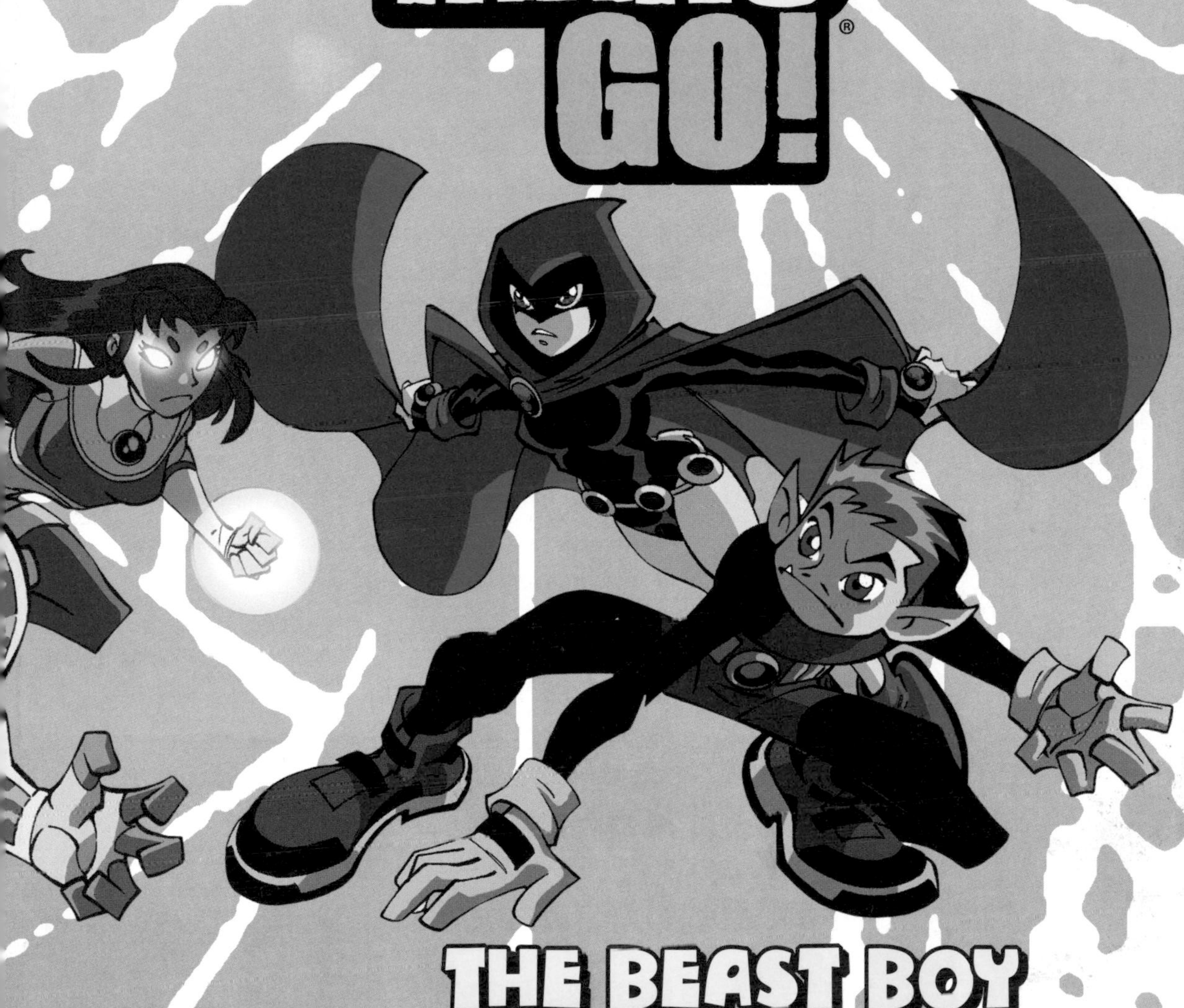

THE BEAST BOY WHO CRIED WOLF

J. Torres..writer
Todd Nauck & Lary Stucker.......................artists
Brad Anderson...colourist
Jared K. Fletcher..letterer

TEEN TITANS GO!

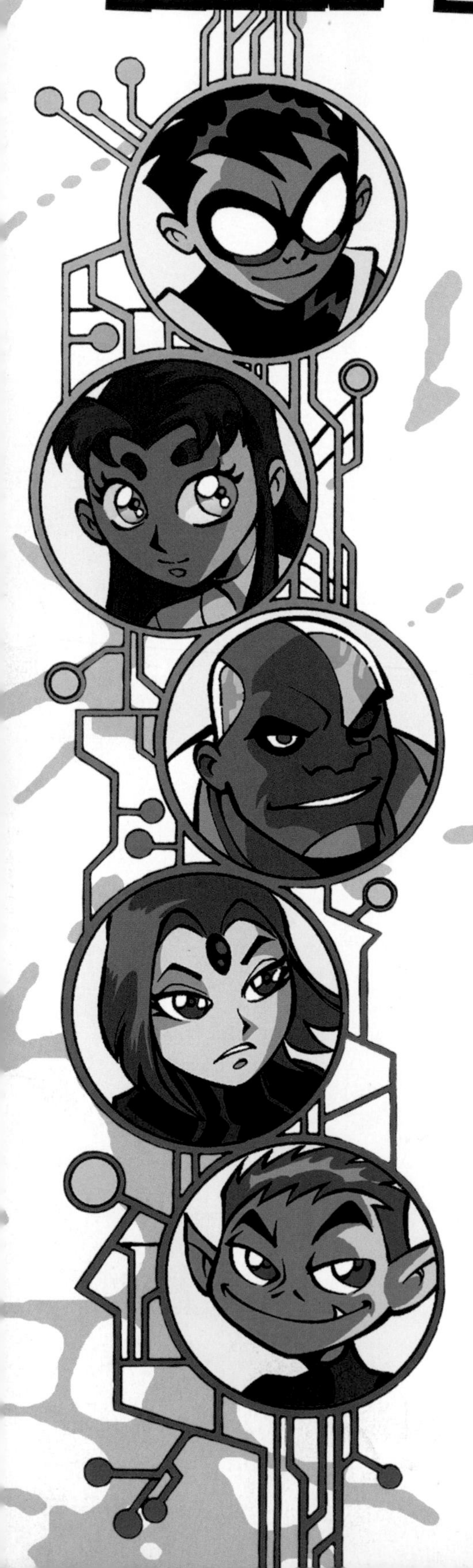

ROBIN

REAL NAME: Dick Grayson

BIO: The perfectionist leader of the group has one main complaint about his teammates: the other Titans just won't do what he says. As the partner of Batman, Robin is a talented acrobat, martial artist, and hacker.

STARFIRE

REAL NAME: Princess Koriand'r

BIO: Formerly a warrior Princess of the now-destroyed planet Tamaran, Starfire found a new home on Earth, and a new family in the Teen Titans.

CYBORG

REAL NAME: Victor Stone

BIO: Cyborg is a laid-back half teen, half robot who's more interested in eating pizza and playing video games than fighting crime.

RAVEN

REAL NAME: Raven

BIO: Raven is an Azarathian empath who can teleport and control her "soul-self," which can fight physically as well as act as Raven's eyes and ears away from her body.

BEAST BOY

REAL NAME: Garfield Logan

BIO: Beast Boy is Cyborg's best bud. He's a slightly dim but lovable loafer who can transform into all sorts of animals [when he's not too busy eating burritos and watching TV]. He's also a vegetarian.

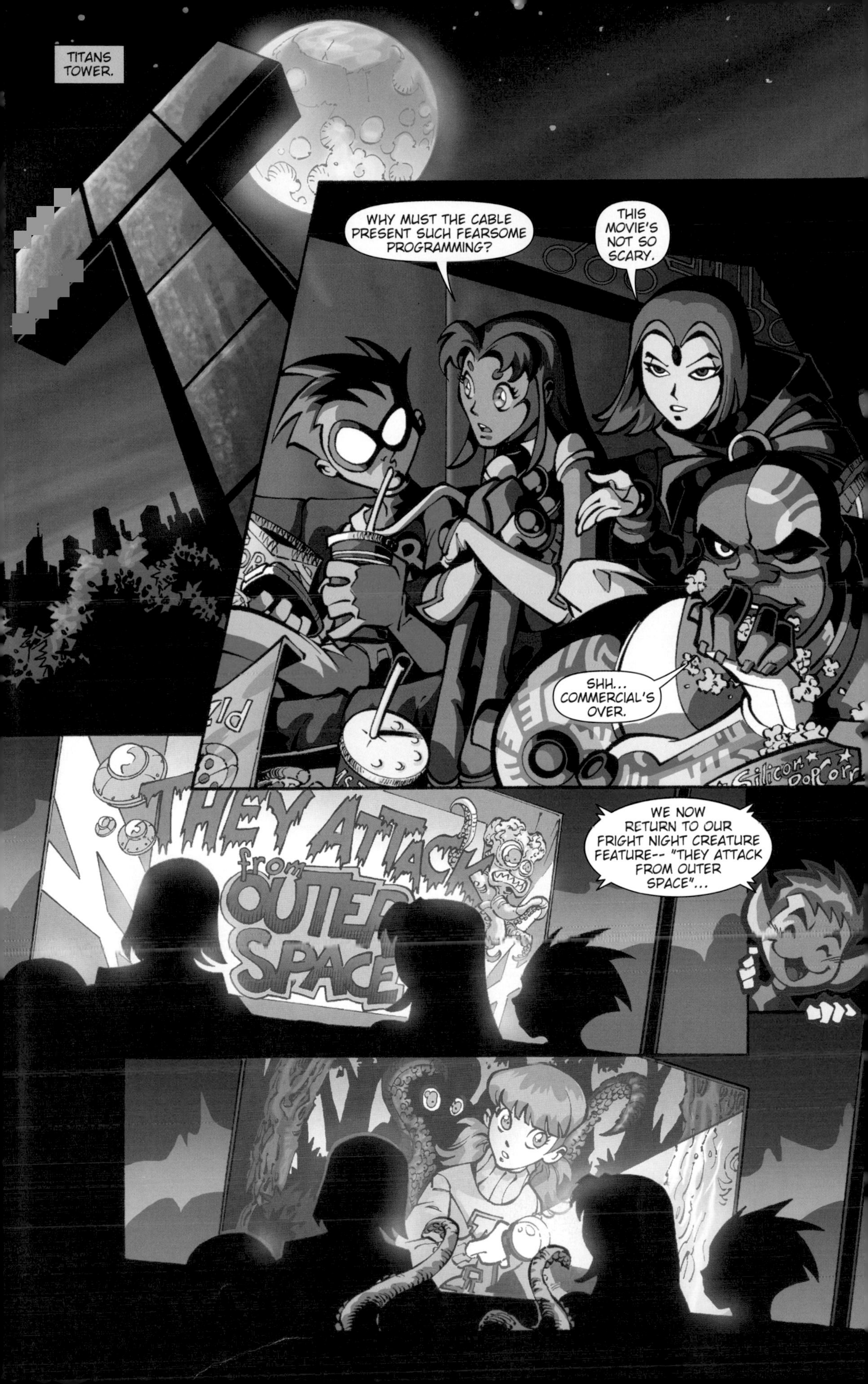
TITANS TOWER.
WHY MUST THE CABLE PRESENT SUCH FEARSOME PROGRAMMING?
THIS MOVIE'S NOT SO SCARY.
SHH... COMMERCIAL'S OVER.
Silicon PopCorn
THEY ATTACK from OUTER SPACE
WE NOW RETURN TO OUR FRIGHT NIGHT CREATURE FEATURE-- "THEY ATTACK FROM OUTER SPACE"...

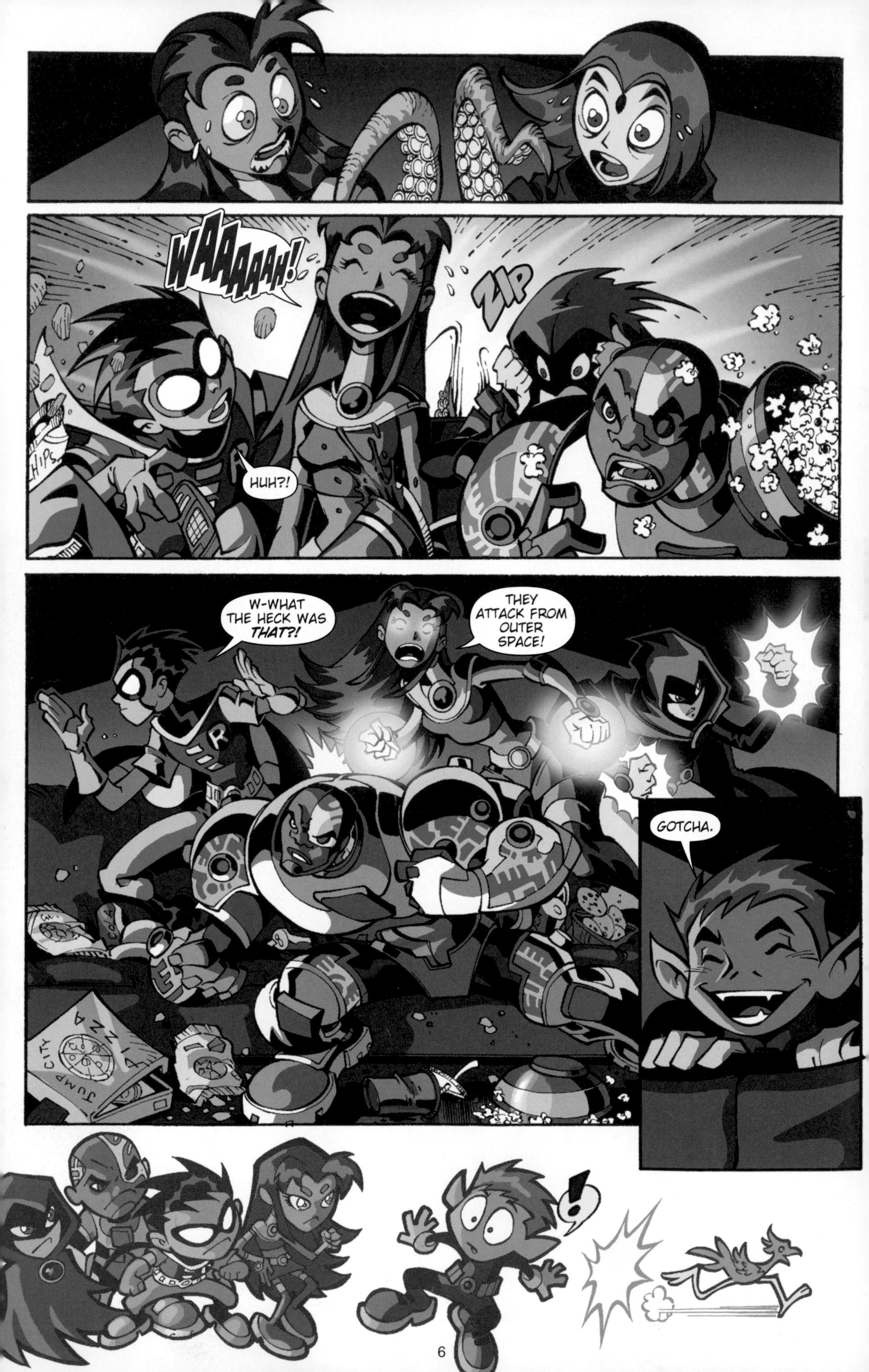
WAAAAAAH!
ZIP
HUH?!
CHIPS
W-WHAT THE HECK WAS THAT?!
THEY ATTACK FROM OUTER SPACE!
GOTCHA.
JUMP CITY PIZZA
!

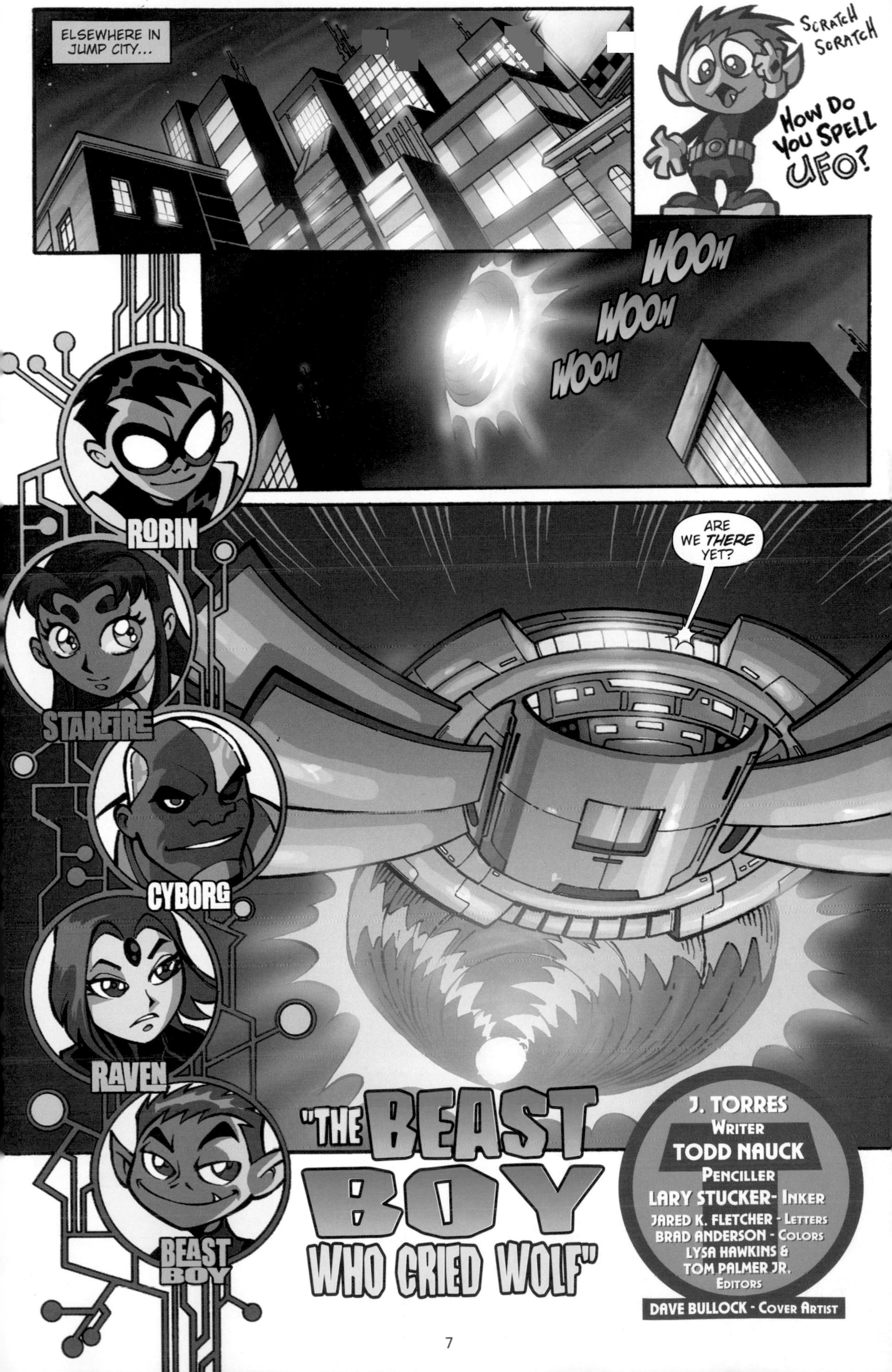
ELSEWHERE IN JUMP CITY...
SCRATCH SCRATCH
HOW DO YOU SPELL UFO?
WOOM WOOM WOOM
ARE WE THERE YET?
ROBIN
STARFIRE
CYBORG
RAVEN
BEAST BOY
"THE BEAST BOY WHO CRIED WOLF"
J. TORRES WRITER
TODD NAUCK PENCILLER
LARY STUCKER- INKER
JARED K. FLETCHER - LETTERS
BRAD ANDERSON - COLORS
LYSA HAWKINS & TOM PALMER JR. EDITORS
DAVE BULLOCK - COVER ARTIST

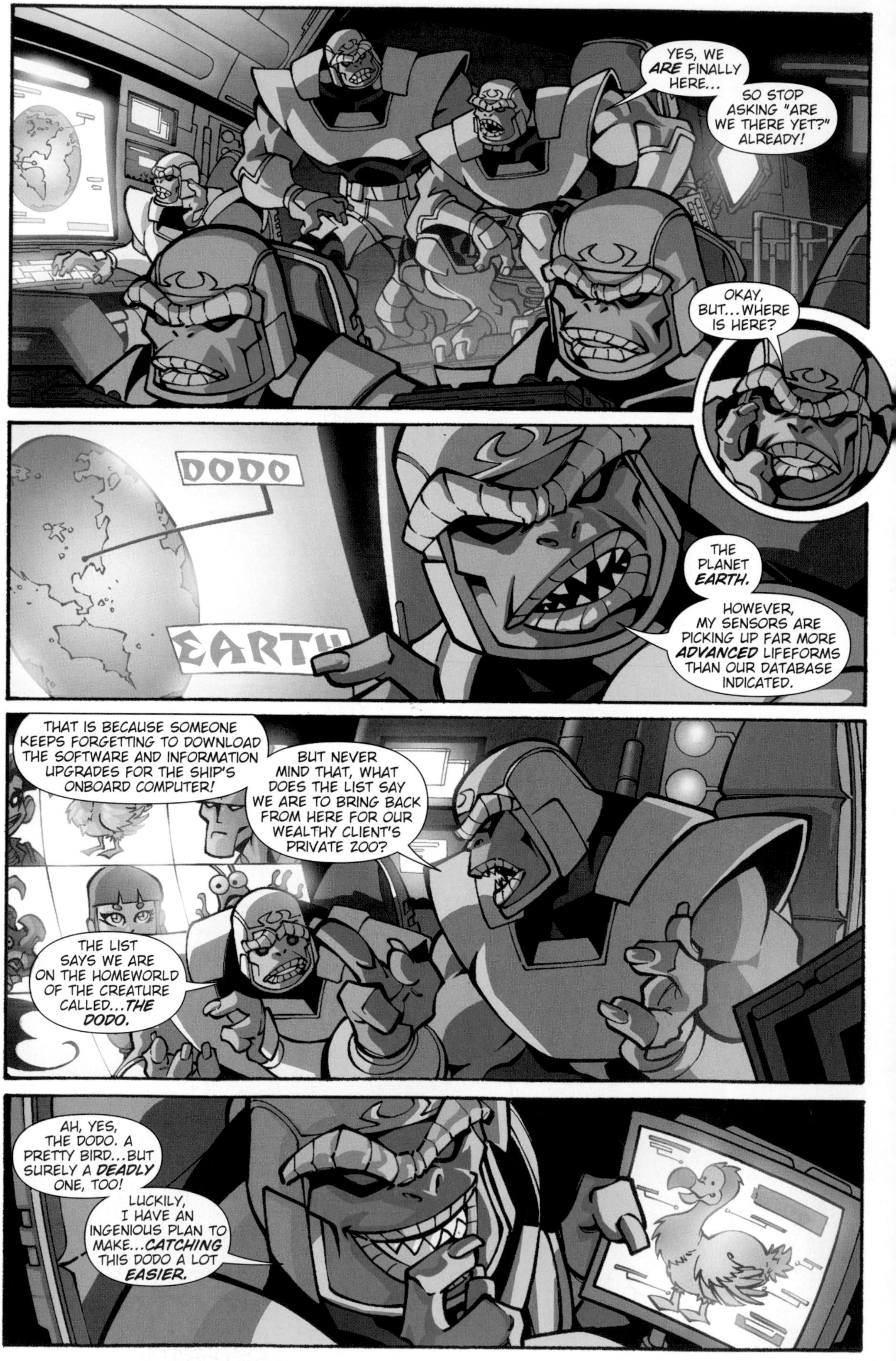
YES, WE ARE FINALLY HERE...
SO STOP ASKING "ARE WE THERE YET?" ALREADY!
OKAY, BUT...WHERE IS HERE?
DODO
EARTH
THE PLANET EARTH.
HOWEVER, MY SENSORS ARE PICKING UP FAR MORE ADVANCED LIFEFORMS THAN OUR DATABASE INDICATED.
THAT IS BECAUSE SOMEONE KEEPS FORGETTING TO DOWNLOAD THE SOFTWARE AND INFORMATION UPGRADES FOR THE SHIP'S ONBOARD COMPUTER!
BUT NEVER MIND THAT, WHAT DOES THE LIST SAY WE ARE TO BRING BACK FROM HERE FOR OUR WEALTHY CLIENT'S PRIVATE ZOO?
THE LIST SAYS WE ARE ON THE HOMEWORLD OF THE CREATURE CALLED...THE DODO.
AH, YES, THE DODO. A PRETTY BIRD...BUT SURELY A DEADLY ONE, TOO!
LUCKILY, I HAVE AN INGENIOUS PLAN TO MAKE...CATCHING THIS DODO A LOT EASIER.

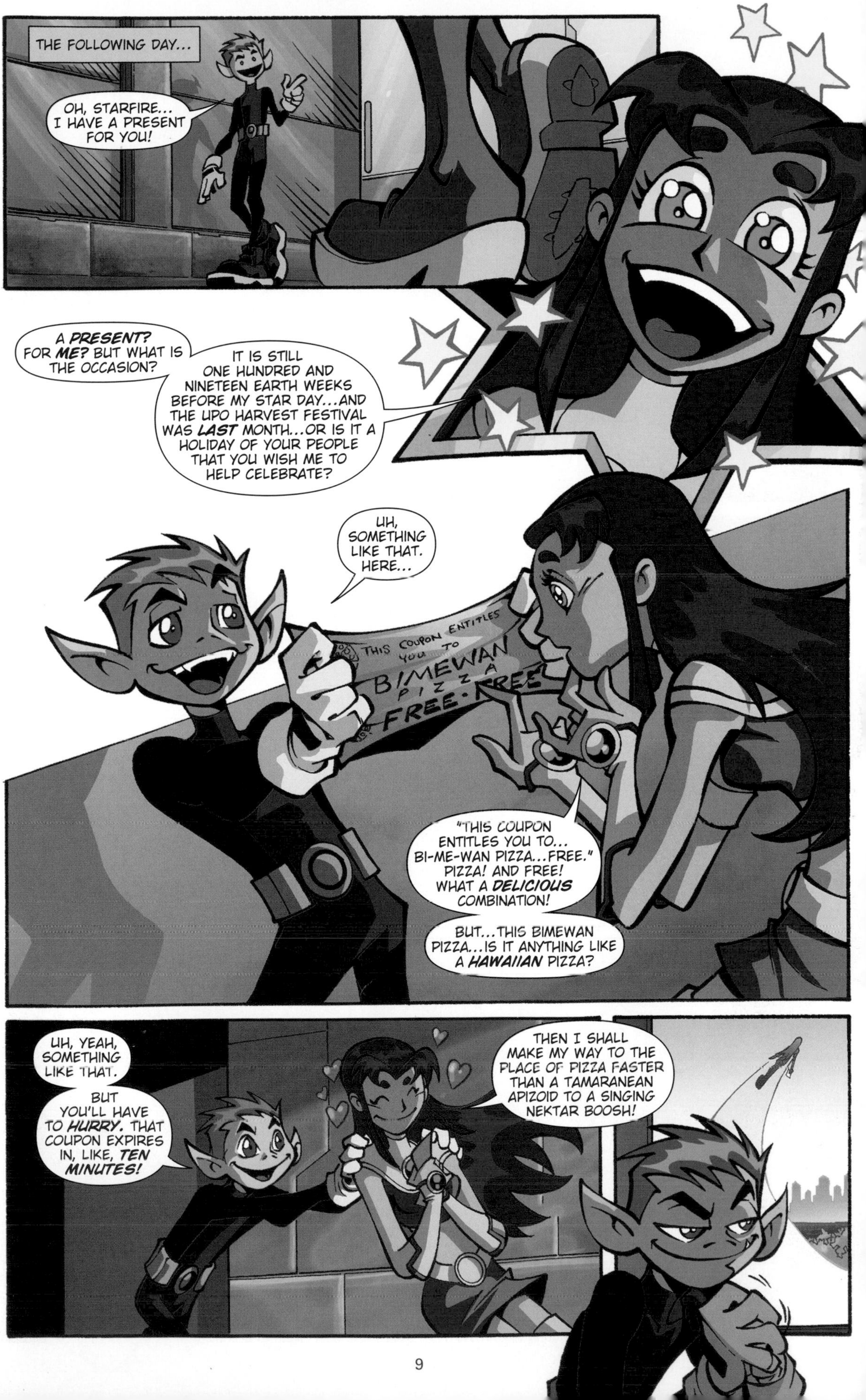
THE FOLLOWING DAY...
OH, STARFIRE... I HAVE A PRESENT FOR YOU!
A PRESENT? FOR ME? BUT WHAT IS THE OCCASION?
IT IS STILL ONE HUNDRED AND NINETEEN EARTH WEEKS BEFORE MY STAR DAY...AND THE UPO HARVEST FESTIVAL WAS LAST MONTH...OR IS IT A HOLIDAY OF YOUR PEOPLE THAT YOU WISH ME TO HELP CELEBRATE?
UH, SOMETHING LIKE THAT. HERE...
THIS COUPON ENTITLES YOU TO BIMEWAN PIZZA FREE · FREE
"THIS COUPON ENTITLES YOU TO... BI-ME-WAN PIZZA...FREE." PIZZA! AND FREE! WHAT A DELICIOUS COMBINATION!
BUT...THIS BIMEWAN PIZZA...IS IT ANYTHING LIKE A HAWAIIAN PIZZA?
UH, YEAH, SOMETHING LIKE THAT.
BUT YOU'LL HAVE TO HURRY. THAT COUPON EXPIRES IN, LIKE, TEN MINUTES!
THEN I SHALL MAKE MY WAY TO THE PLACE OF PIZZA FASTER THAN A TAMARANEAN APIZOID TO A SINGING NEKTAR BOOSH!

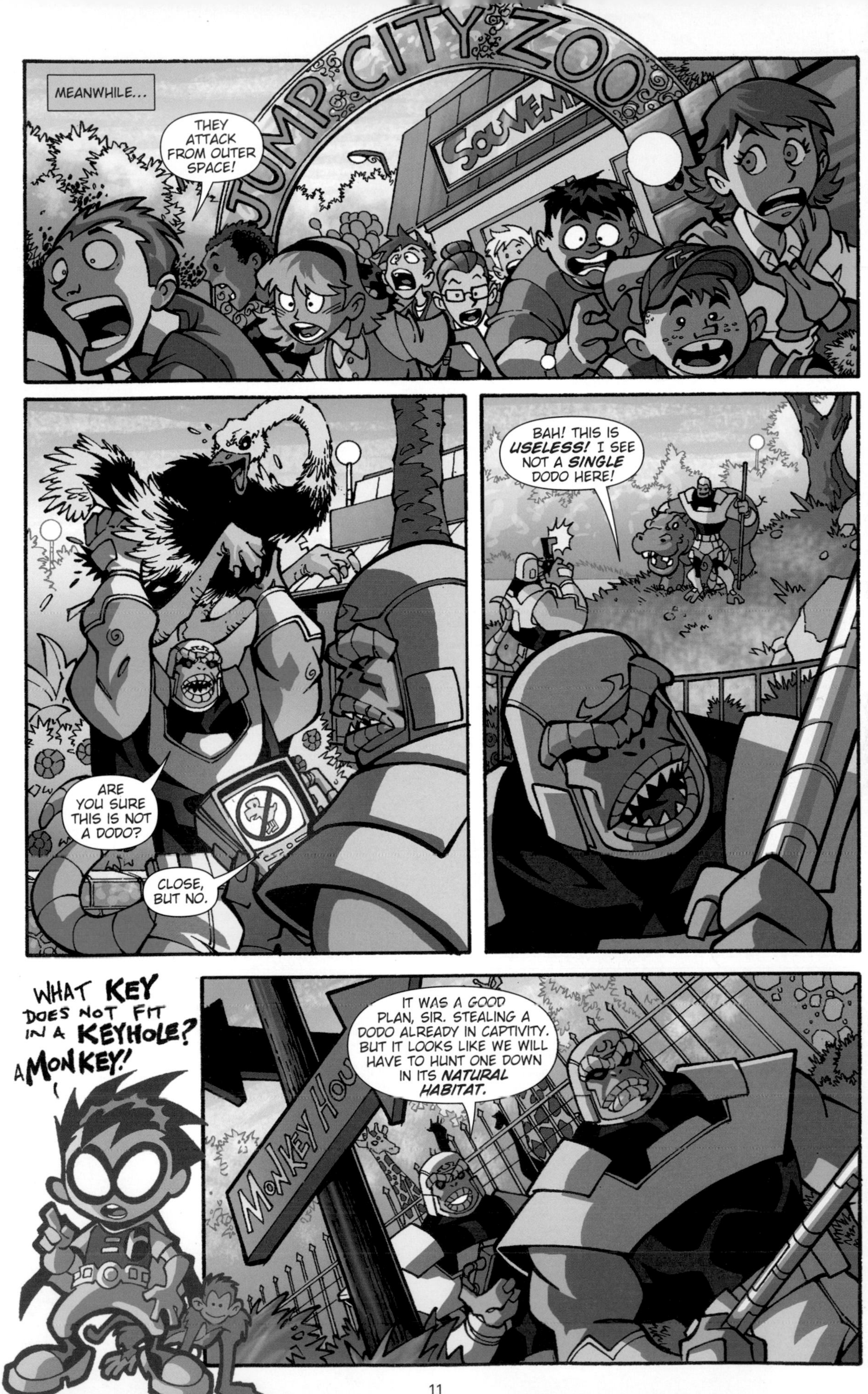

JUMP CITY ZOO
MEANWHILE...
THEY ATTACK FROM OUTER SPACE!
SOUVENI
BAH! THIS IS USELESS! I SEE NOT A SINGLE DODO HERE!
ARE YOU SURE THIS IS NOT A DODO?
CLOSE, BUT NO.
WHAT KEY DOES NOT FIT IN A KEYHOLE? A MONKEY!
MONKEY HOU
IT WAS A GOOD PLAN, SIR. STEALING A DODO ALREADY IN CAPTIVITY. BUT IT LOOKS LIKE WE WILL HAVE TO HUNT ONE DOWN IN ITS NATURAL HABITAT.

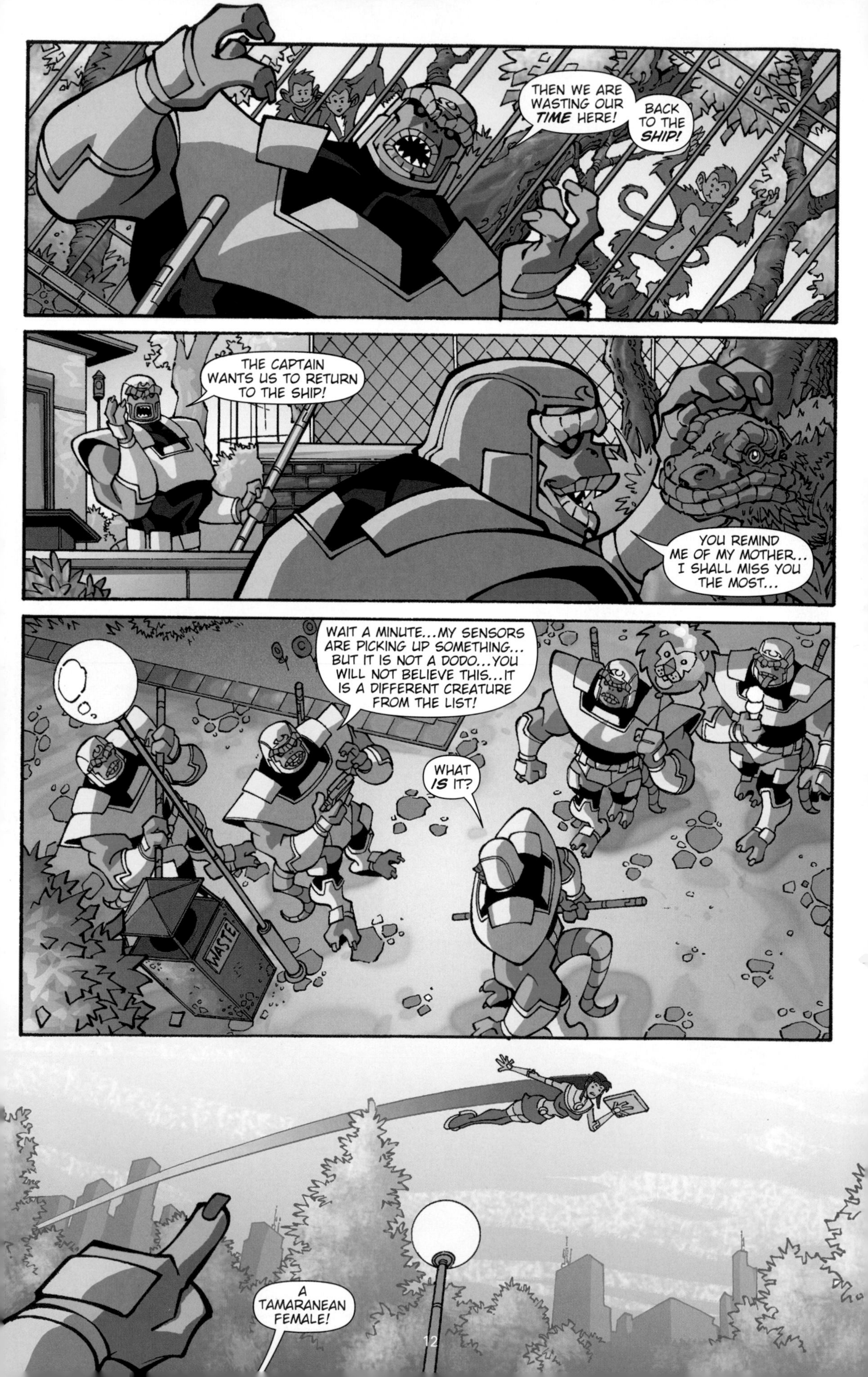
THEN WE ARE WASTING OUR *TIME* HERE!
BACK TO THE *SHIP!*
THE CAPTAIN WANTS US TO RETURN TO THE SHIP!
YOU REMIND ME OF MY MOTHER... I SHALL MISS YOU THE MOST...
WAIT A MINUTE...MY SENSORS ARE PICKING UP SOMETHING... BUT IT IS NOT A DODO...YOU WILL NOT BELIEVE THIS...IT IS A DIFFERENT CREATURE FROM THE LIST!
WHAT *IS* IT?
WASTE
A TAMARANEAN FEMALE!

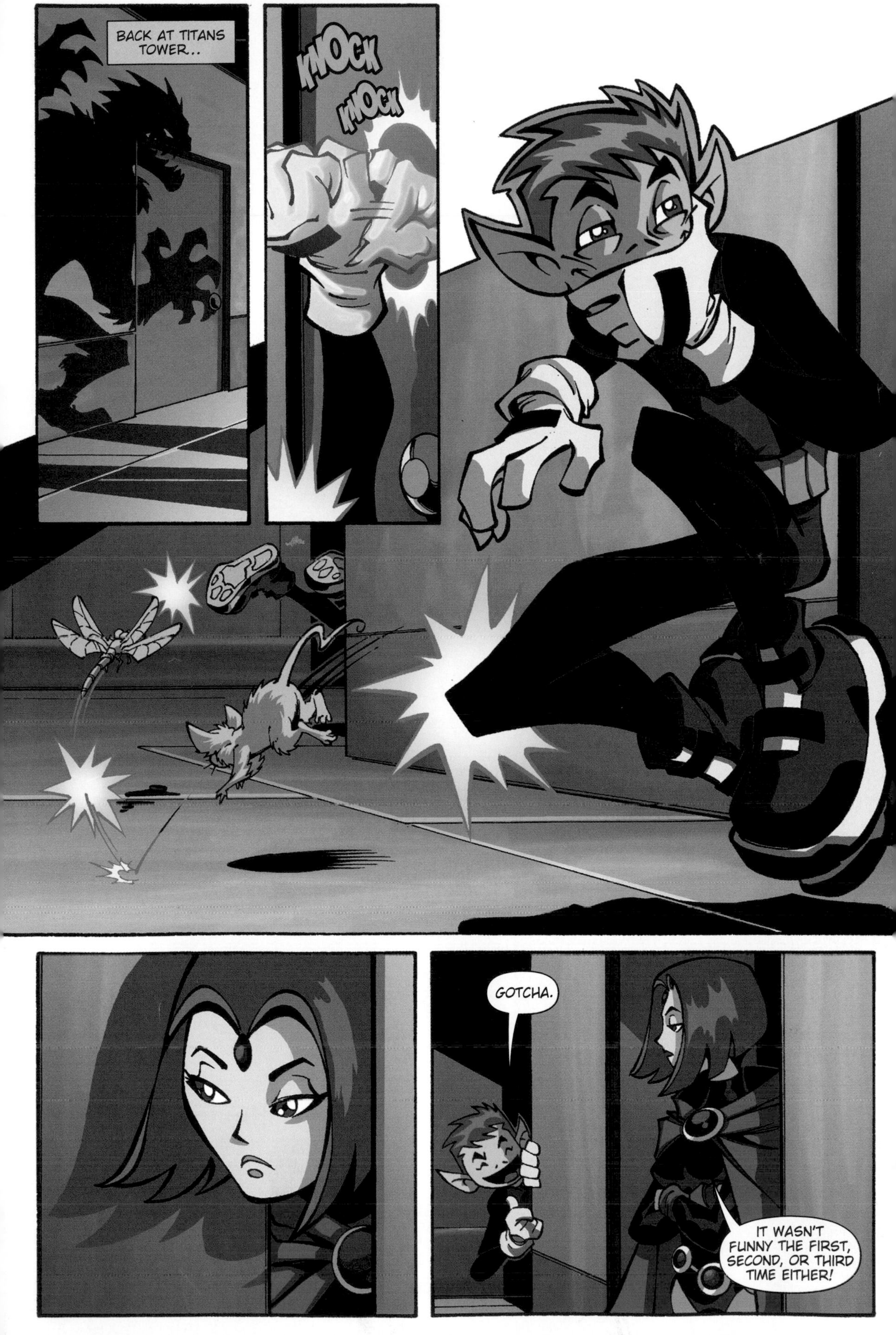
BACK AT TITANS TOWER...
KNOCK
KNOCK
GOTCHA.
IT WASN'T FUNNY THE FIRST, SECOND, OR THIRD TIME EITHER!

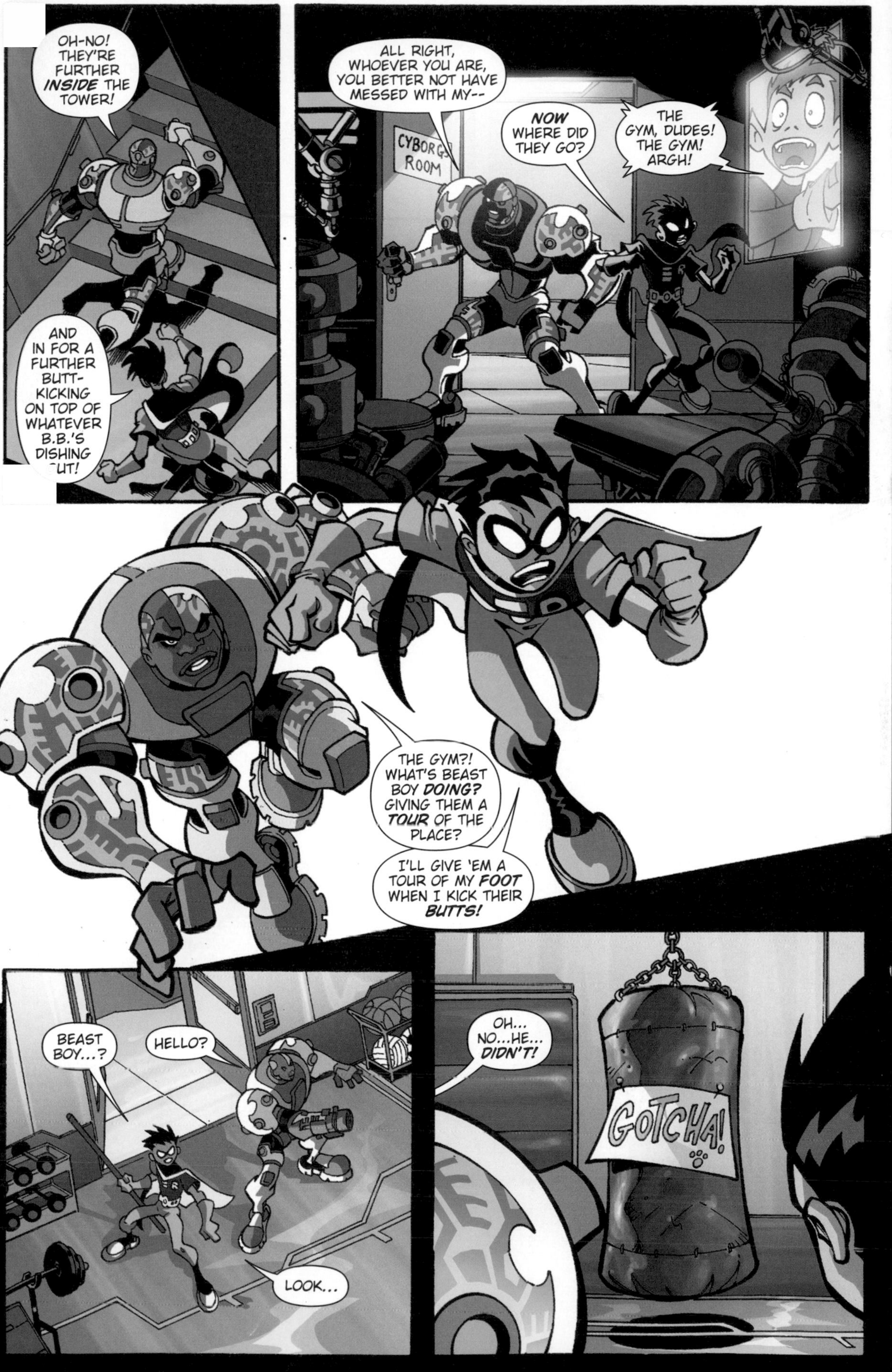
OH-NO! THEY'RE FURTHER INSIDE THE TOWER!
AND IN FOR A FURTHER BUTT-KICKING ON TOP OF WHATEVER B.B.'S DISHING OUT!
ALL RIGHT, WHOEVER YOU ARE, YOU BETTER NOT HAVE MESSED WITH MY--
CYBORG'S ROOM
NOW WHERE DID THEY GO?
THE GYM, DUDES! THE GYM! ARGH!
THE GYM?! WHAT'S BEAST BOY DOING? GIVING THEM A TOUR OF THE PLACE?
I'LL GIVE 'EM A TOUR OF MY FOOT WHEN I KICK THEIR BUTTS!
BEAST BOY...?
HELLO?
LOOK...
OH... NO...HE... DIDN'T!
GOTCHA!

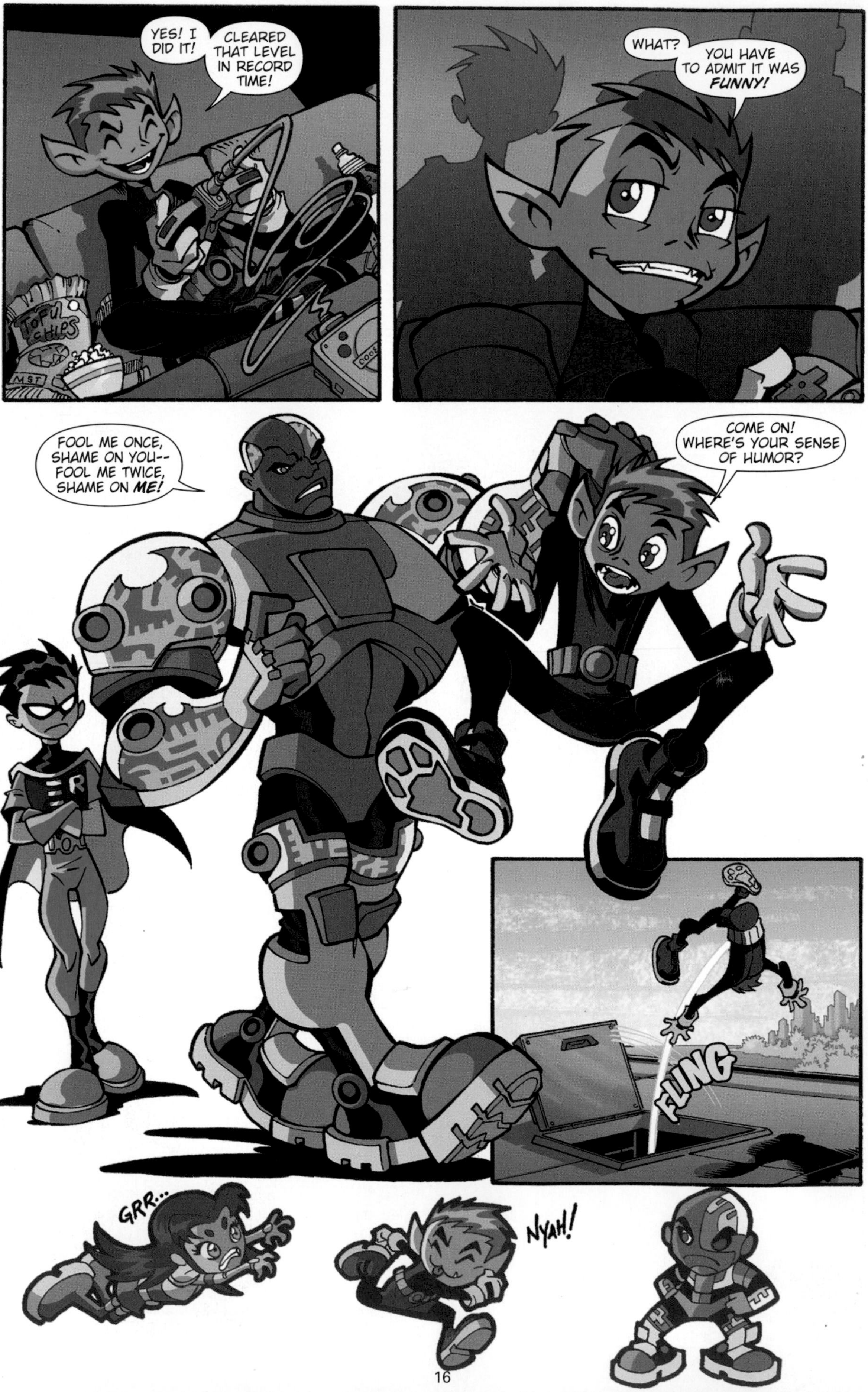

YES! I DID IT!
CLEARED THAT LEVEL IN RECORD TIME!
TOFU CHIPS
WHAT?
YOU HAVE TO ADMIT IT WAS FUNNY!
FOOL ME ONCE, SHAME ON YOU-- FOOL ME TWICE, SHAME ON ME!
COME ON! WHERE'S YOUR SENSE OF HUMOR?
FLING
GRR...
NYAH!

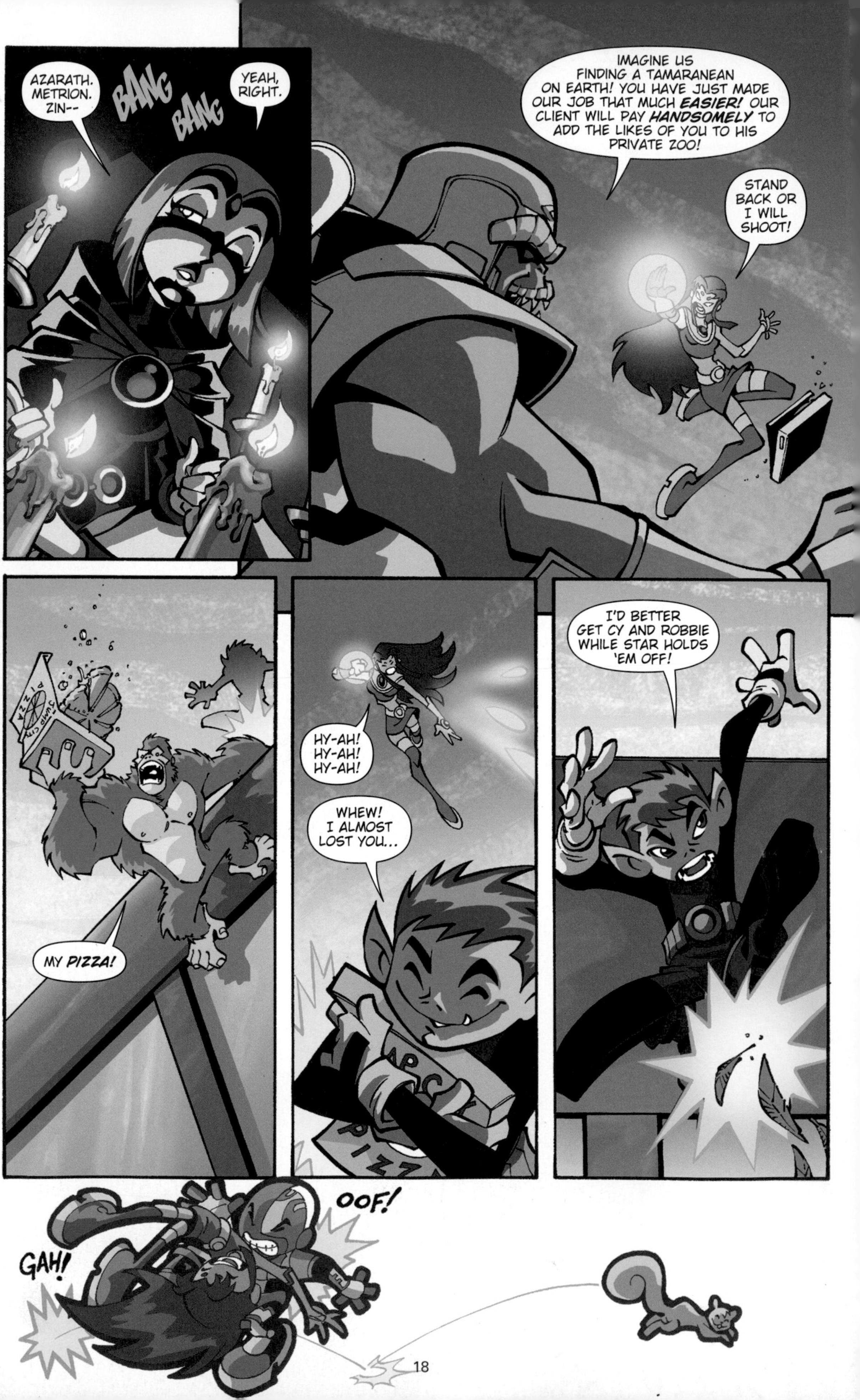
AZARATH. METRION. ZIN--
BANG BANG
YEAH, RIGHT.
IMAGINE US FINDING A TAMARANEAN ON EARTH! YOU HAVE JUST MADE OUR JOB THAT MUCH EASIER! OUR CLIENT WILL PAY HANDSOMELY TO ADD THE LIKES OF YOU TO HIS PRIVATE ZOO!
STAND BACK OR I WILL SHOOT!
MY PIZZA!
HY-AH! HY-AH! HY-AH!
WHEW! I ALMOST LOST YOU...
I'D BETTER GET CY AND ROBBIE WHILE STAR HOLDS 'EM OFF!
OOF!
GAH!

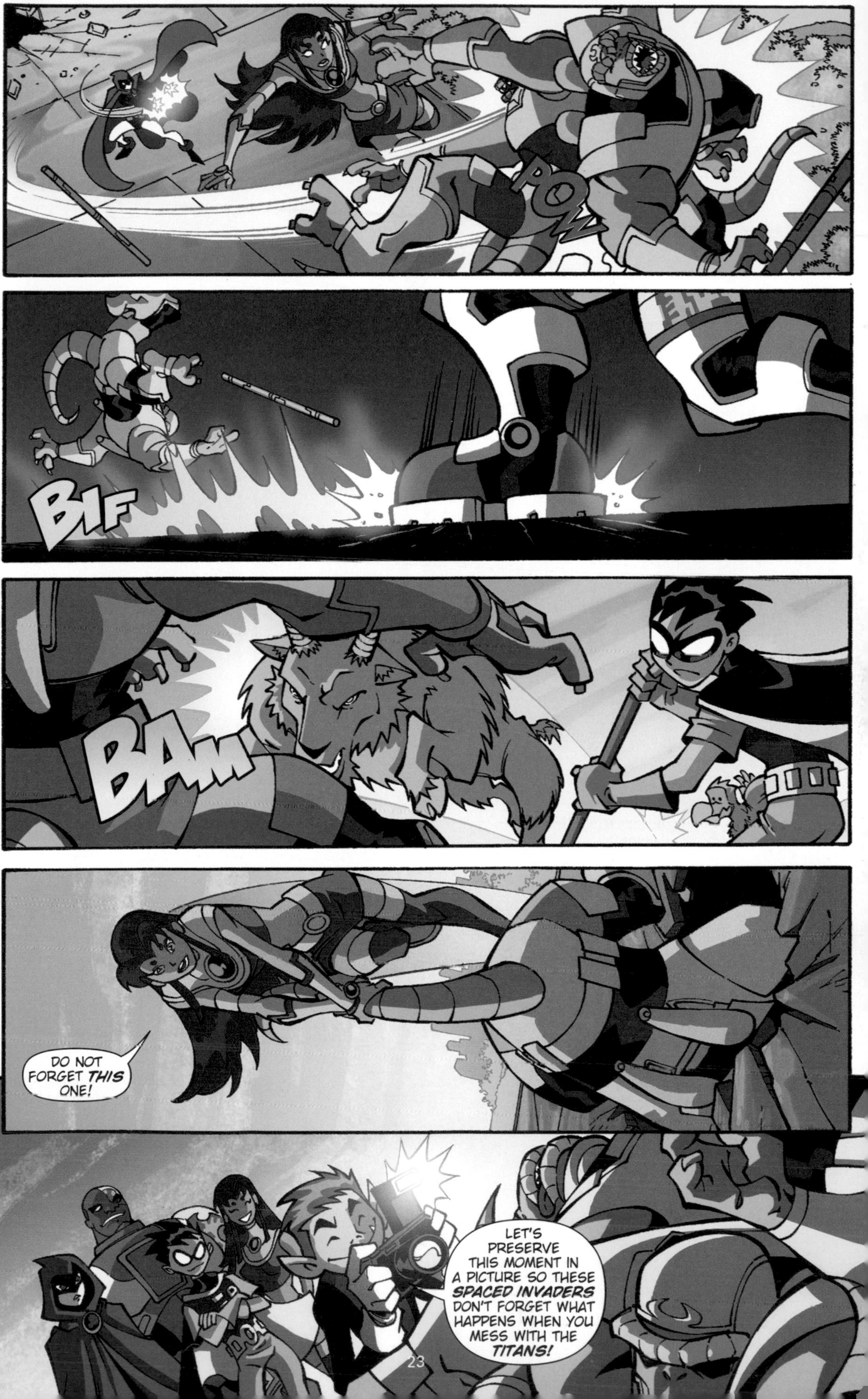
POW
BIF
BAM
DO NOT FORGET THIS ONE!
LET'S PRESERVE THIS MOMENT IN A PICTURE SO THESE SPACED INVADERS DON'T FORGET WHAT HAPPENS WHEN YOU MESS WITH THE TITANS!

CREATORS

J. TORRES WRITER

J. Torres won the Shuster Award for Outstanding Writer for his work on Batman: Legends of the Dark Knight, Love As a Foreign Language, and Teen Titans Go! He is also the writer of the Eisner Award nominated Alison Dare and the YALSA listed Days Like This and Lola: A Ghost Story. Other comic book credits include Avatar: The Last Airbender, Batman: The Brave and the Bold, Legion of Super-Heroes in the 31st Century, Ninja Scroll, Wonder Girl, Wonder Woman, and WALL-E: Recharge.

TODD NAUCK ARTIST

Todd Nauck is an American comic book artist and writer. Nauck is most notable for his work on Young Justice, Teen Titans Go!, and his own creation, Wildguard.

GLOSSARY

captivity – that state of being imprisoned, confined, or enslaved

database – the information that is organized and stored in a computer

detain – hold somebody back when they want to go or leave

dodo – an extinct bird that was clumsy and unable to fly

expire – die or end

extinct – has died out, or is no longer in existence

habitat – natural environment

ingenious – clever or creative

intruder – someone who enters an area without permission

invader – person who enters forcefully as an enemy

override – overrule, or have final say over something

VISUAL QUESTIONS & PROMPTS

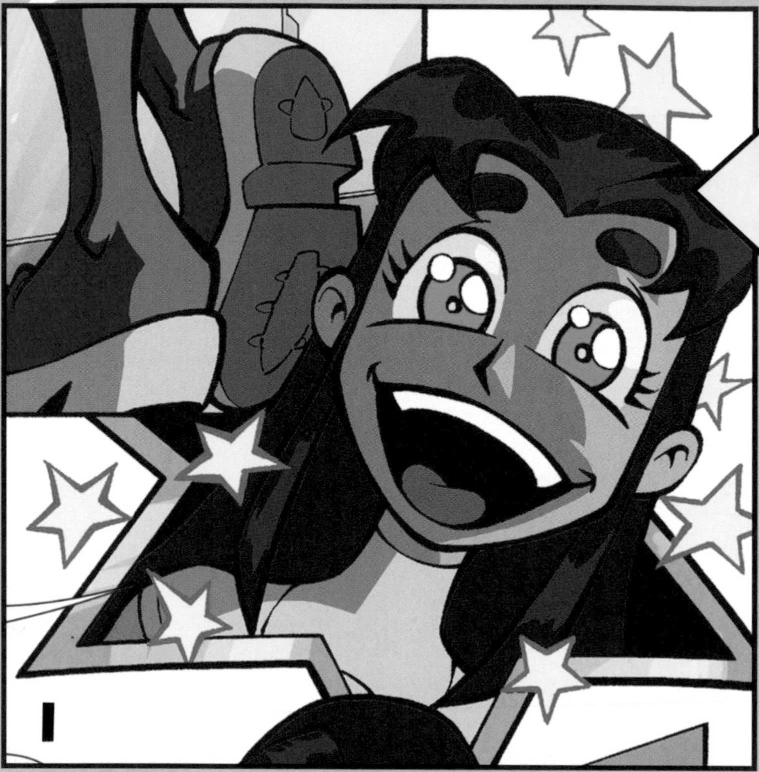
1

1. On page 9, Starfire is seen with stars circling her head. Based on the surrounding pages, what do you think the stars mean? How does she feel, and why?

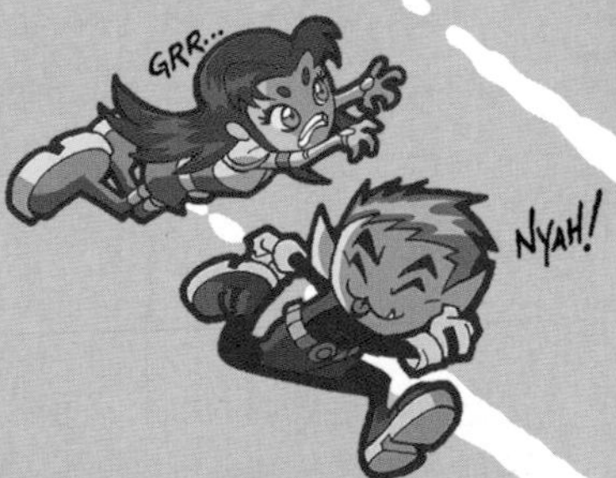
GRR...
NYAH!

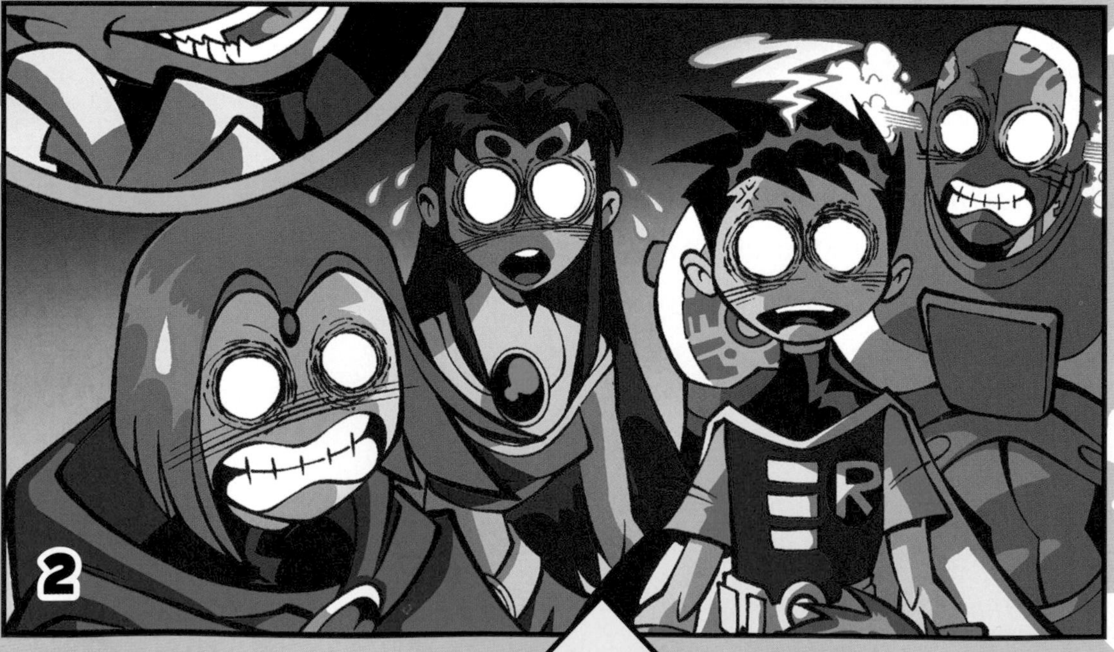
2

2. In this panel, we see the Teen Titans react to Beast Boy's behaviour on page 26. Why did they react the way they did in this panel?

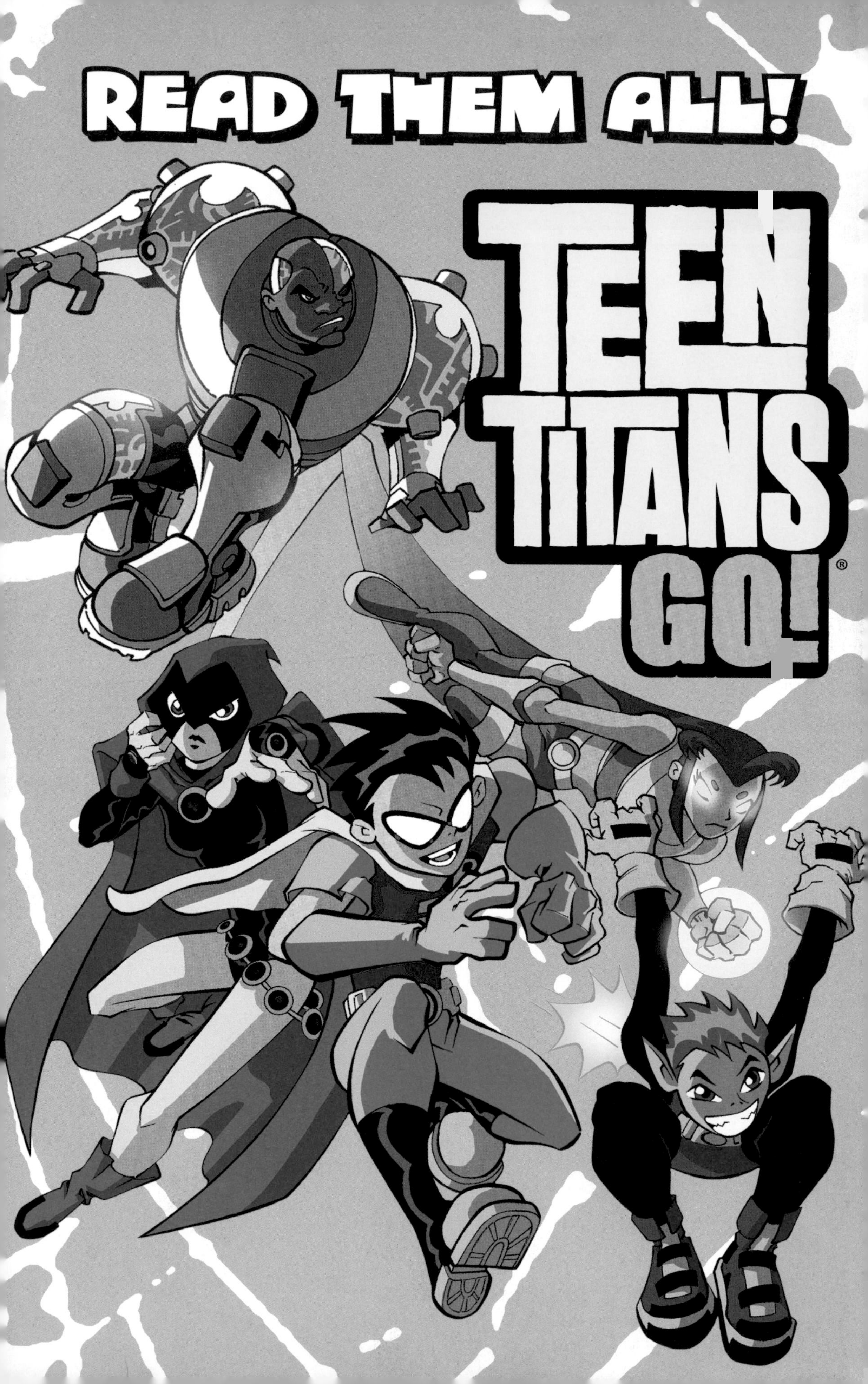
READ THEM ALL!
TEEN TITANS GO!®

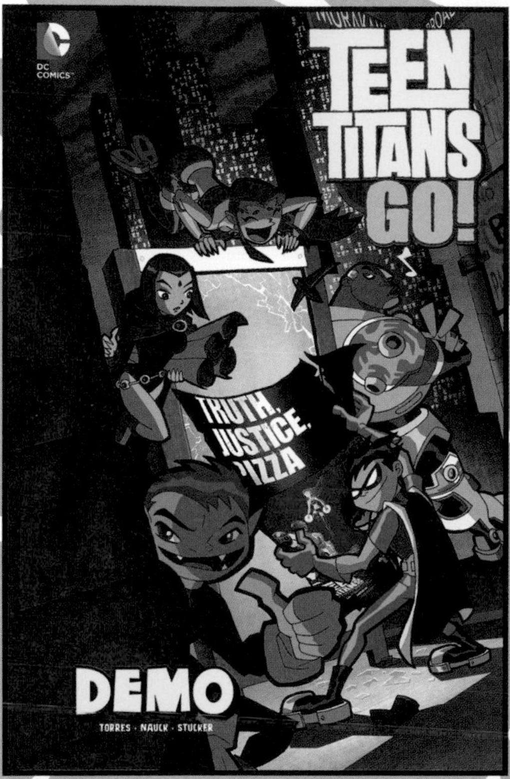
DC COMICS
TEEN TITANS GO!
TRUTH, JUSTICE, PIZZA
DEMO
TORRES · NAUCK · STUCKER

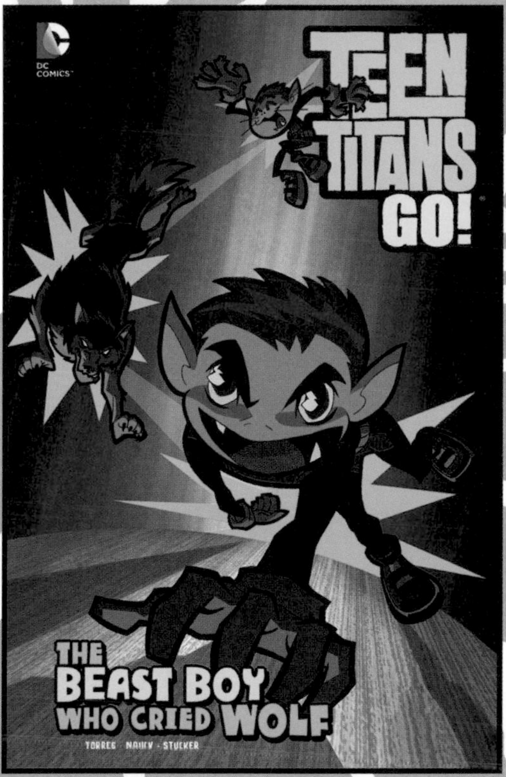
DC COMICS
TEEN TITANS GO!
THE BEAST BOY WHO CRIED WOLF
TORRES · NAUCK · STUCKER

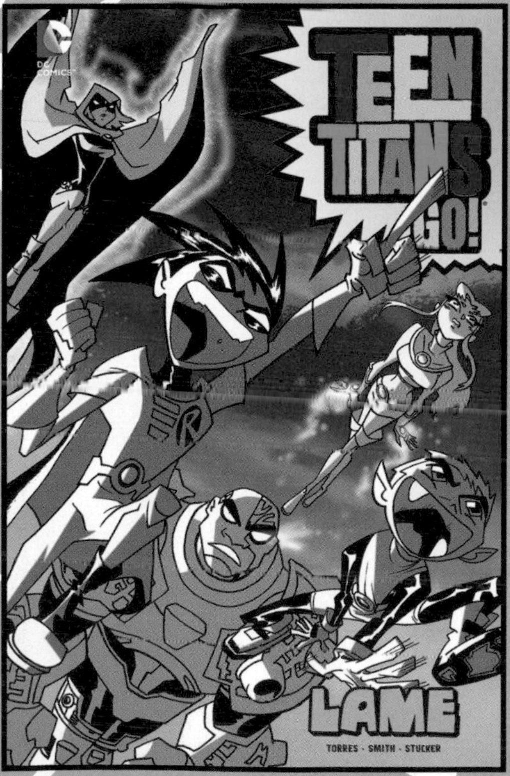
DC COMICS
TEEN TITANS GO!
LAME
TORRES · SMITH · STUCKER

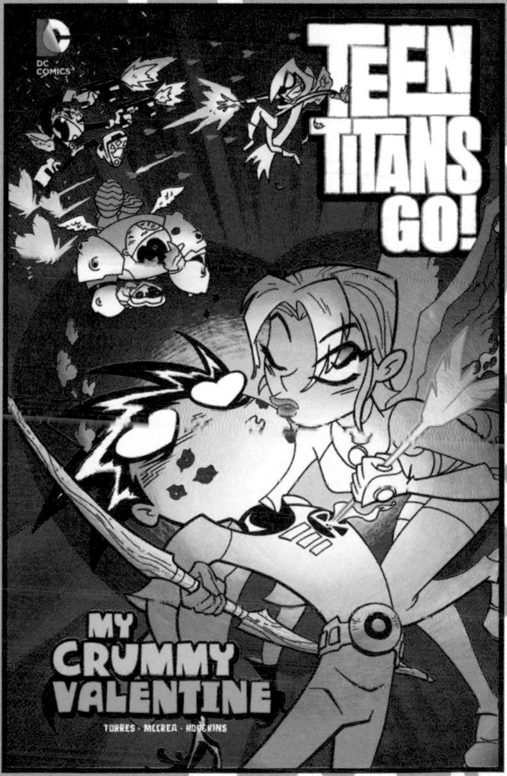
DC COMICS
TEEN TITANS GO!
MY CRUMMY VALENTINE
TORRES · MCCREA · HODGKINS

Raintree

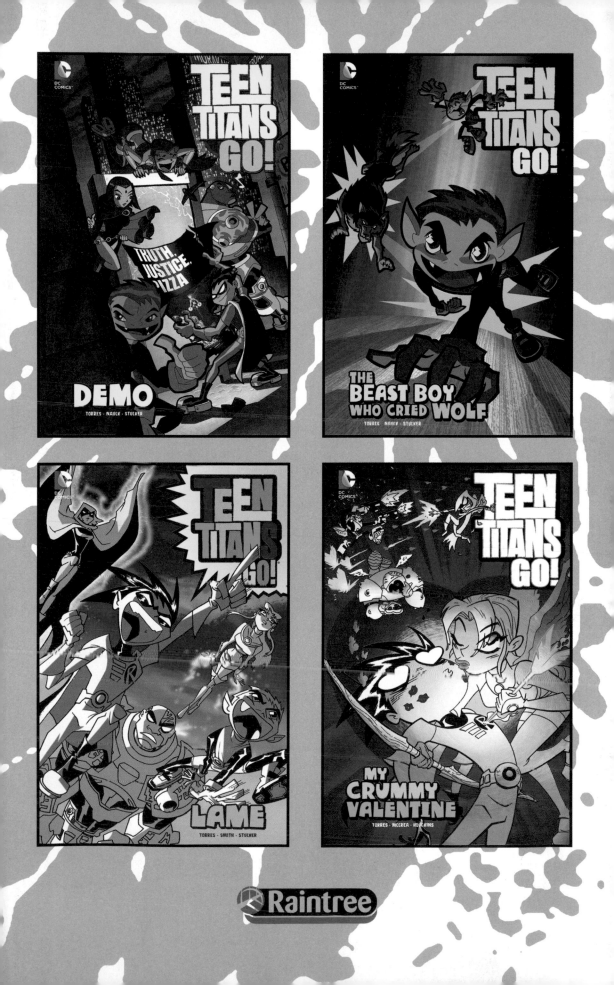

TEEN TITANS GO!®

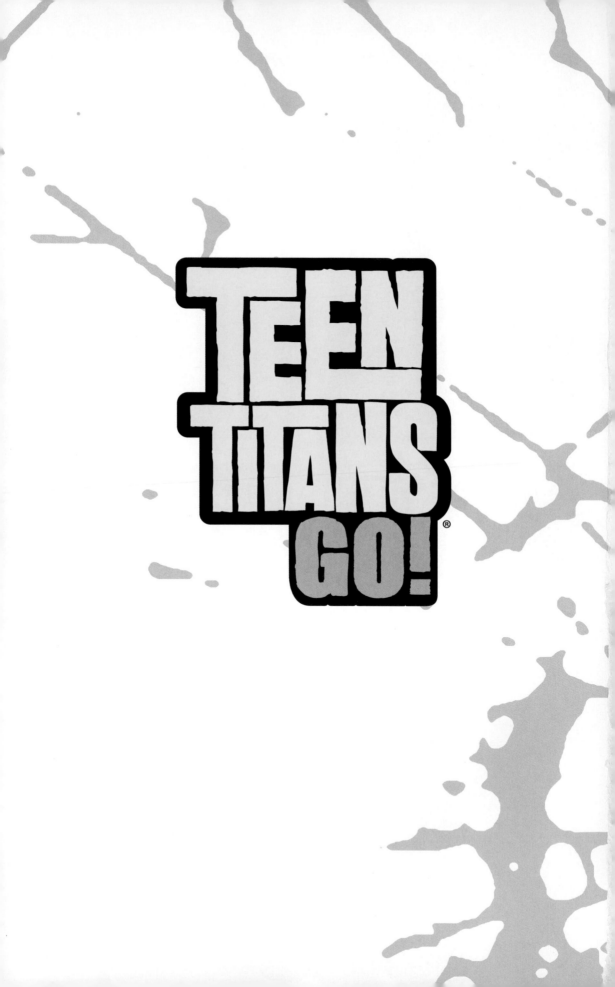